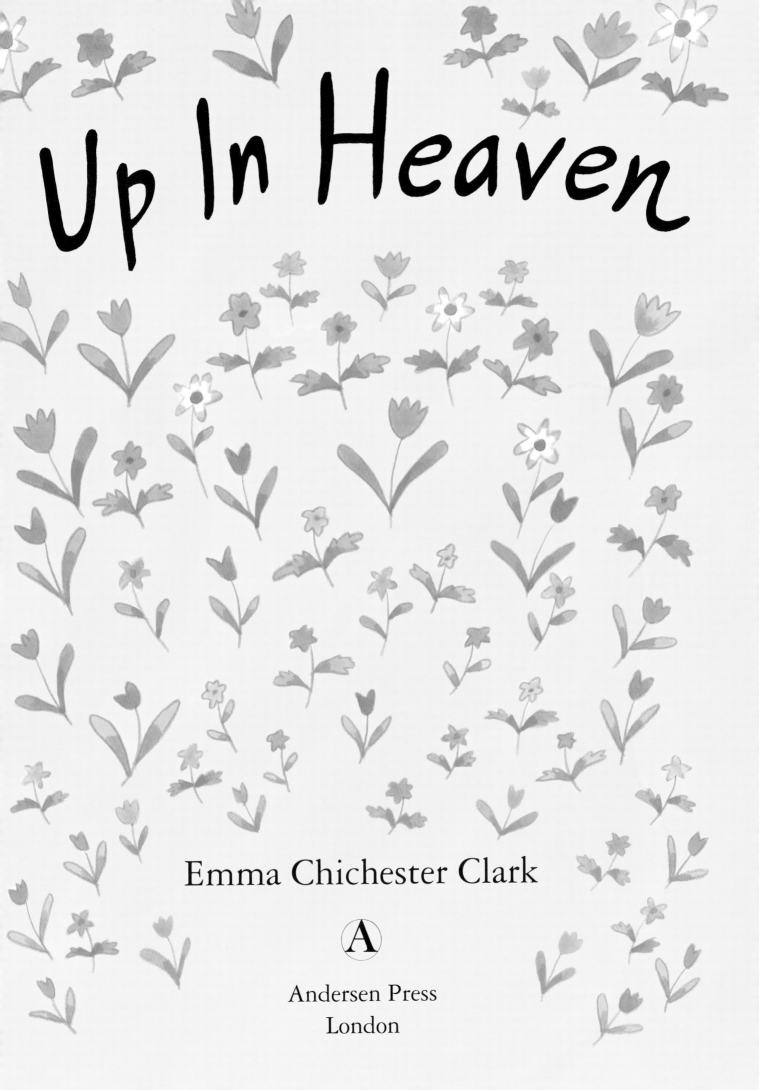

Up In Heaven

Emma Chichester Clark

Andersen Press
London

In memory of
Tarquin, Grace, Fergus,
Honey, Daisy, Brocky,
Zany, Gismo,
&
Mistletoe

Copyright © 2003 by Emma Chichester Clark
The rights of Emma Chichester Clark to be identified as the author and illustrator
of this work have been asserted by her in accordance with the Copyright, Designs and Patents Act, 1988.
First published in Great Britain in 2003 by Andersen Press Ltd., 20 Vauxhall Bridge Road, London SW1V 2SA.
Published in Australia by Random House Australia Pty., 20 Alfred Street, Milsons Point, Sydney, NSW 2061.
All rights reserved. Colour separated in Switzerland by Photolitho AG, Zürich.
Printed and bound in Italy by Grafiche AZ., Verona.

10   9   8   7   6   5   4   3   2   1

British Library Cataloguing in Publication Data available.

ISBN 1 84270 046 4

This book has been printed on acid-free paper

Daisy was devoted to Arthur,
but she couldn't keep up with him anymore.

She was slowing down because she was very, very old.
And she didn't always feel well.

One night, she went to sleep, as usual, but when she woke up . . .

. . . she was in heaven!
It was lovely, up in heaven.

There were beautiful gardens and lakes to swim in.
The sun shone all the time.

Daisy didn't feel tired anymore.
She could run as fast as she used to when she was young.

And she found lots of new and old friends.

Daisy could see everything from up there.
"I wish I could tell Arthur about it," she thought.

She could see him and his parents in the garden.
They looked sad.

She watched them having tea.

And she saw Arthur crying when he went to bed.

"What shall I do?" she asked her friends.
"Send him dreams," they answered.

In the first dream, Daisy made
a picture to show Arthur
where heaven was.

She saw Arthur telling his mother about it in the morning.

But in the afternoon he was sad and quiet again.

In the next dream, Daisy showed Arthur how beautiful
it was in heaven, and she showed him all her friends.

Arthur seemed more cheerful the next day,

but Daisy could see he was missing her.

"How can I help him?" she asked her friends.

"Give him a new puppy dream," they answered.

"Show you don't mind."

That night, Daisy sent a dream of a little puppy.
She watched Arthur smiling in his sleep.

At breakfast, she listened to Arthur telling his parents.

Then she watched them driving out into the countryside,
where the new puppies were.

Daisy watched Arthur choose his puppy.

And she knew that everything was going to be all right.

Now she could really enjoy herself.

It was lovely, up in heaven.

But she still kept an eye on Arthur.
And little Maisy, most of the time.